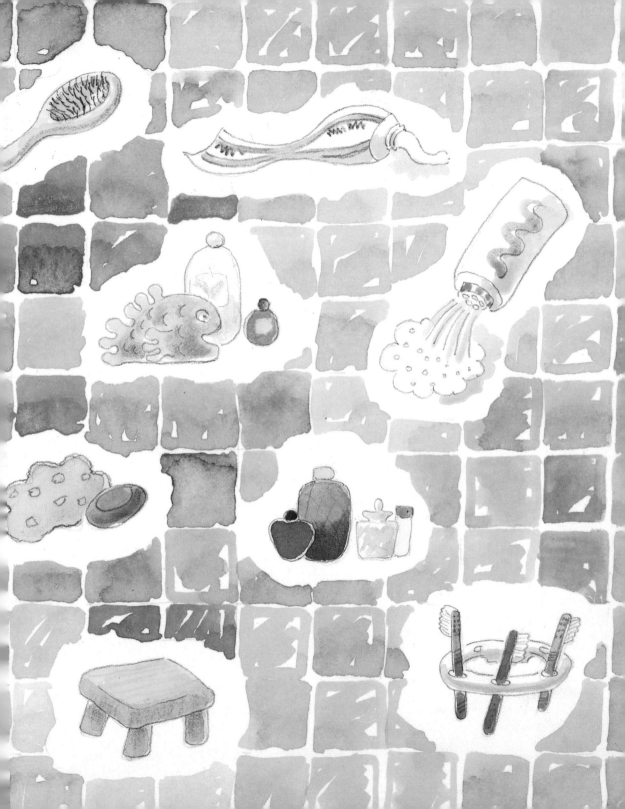

To parents and teachers

We hope you and the children will enjoy reading this story in English or Spanish. The story is simple, but not *simplified,* so that both versions are quite natural. However, there is lots of repetition for practicing pronunciation, for helping develop memory skills, and for reinforcing comprehension.

At the back of the book there is a small picture dictionary with the key words and a basic pronunciation guide to the whole story.

Here are a few suggestions for using the book:

- Read the story aloud in English first, to get to know it. Treat it like any other picture book: look at the pictures, talk about the story, the characters, and so on.

- Then look at the picture dictionary and say the key words in Spanish. Ask the children to say the words out loud, rather than reading them.

- Go back and read the story again, this time in English *and* Spanish. Don't worry if your pronunciation isn't quite correct. Just have fun trying it out. Check the guide at the back of the book, if necessary, but you'll soon pick up how to say the Spanish words.

- When you think you and the children are ready, try reading the story in Spanish only. Ask the children to say it with you. Only ask them to read it if they seem eager to try. The spelling could be confusing and discourage them.

- Above all encourage the children, and give lots of praise. Little children are usually quite unselfconscious and this is excellent for building up confidence in a foreign language.

First edition for the United States, its Dependencies, Canada, and the Philippines published 2000 by Barron's Educational Series, Inc. Text © Copyright 2000 by b small publishing, Surrey, England.

International Standard Book Number 0-7641-5286-6   Library of Congress Catalog Card Number 00-131747
Printed in Hong Kong   987654321

Hurry up, Molly

Apúrate, Molly

Lone Morton

Pictures by Gill Scriven
Spanish by Thessa Judkins

BARRON'S

"Come on Molly, into the bathroom.
Then I'll read you a story," says Dad.

"Vamos Molly, al cuarto de baño.
Después te leeré un cuento", dice papá.

"Carry me, carry me!"
　　　Dad picks Molly up.

"¡Llévame en brazos, llévame en brazos!"
　　　Papá toma a Molly.

"Upside down?"

"¿Cabeza abajo?"

"Over my shoulder?"
"¿Sobre mis hombros?"

"Or on my back?" asks Dad.
"¿O en mi espalda?" pregunta papá.

"Like a baby!" says Molly, laughing.

"¡Como un bebé!" dice Molly, riendo.

"Hurry up Molly," Dad says,
"I'll wait in your bedroom."

"Apúrate, Molly", dice papá.
"Te espero en tu dormitorio".

"Wash your face," he calls,
"Lávate la cara", llama,

"and behind your ears."
"y detrás de las orejas".

"Brush your teeth."

"Cepíllate los dientes".

Molly also brushes her hair…
Molly se cepilla el pelo también…

to the left…
a la izquierda…

…to the right,
…a la derecha,

…over her nose,
…sobre la nariz,

and all on top of her head!
¡y todo encima de la cabeza!

Molly looks in Dad's mirror.
Molly se mira en el espejo de papá.

Her chin is long,
Su mentón es largo,

...her eyes are big,
...sus ojos son grandes,

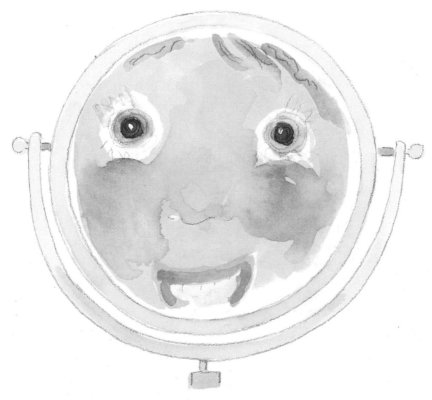

...her cheeks are fat.
...sus mejillas son gorditas.

What a sight!
¡Qué espectáculo!

She puts some talcum powder on her hand, and blows…

Se pone talco en la mano y sopla…

…and blows!
…¡y sopla!

What a mess!
¡Qué lío!

She sprays some perfume
on her neck…

Se echa perfume en el cuello…

…and on her toes.
…y en los dedos del pie.

What a smell!
¡Qué olor!

Molly suddenly remembers her Dad.
"Just coming Dad!" she calls.

Molly se acuerda de repente de su papá.
"¡Ya vengo, papá!" llama.

But guess what Molly finds
in her bedroom?

¿Pero adivina lo que Molly
encuentra en su dormitorio?

"Dad, wake up! I want a story!"
"¡Papá, despiértate! ¡Quiero un cuento!"

But he's fast asleep and snoring.
Pero él está profundamente dormido
y roncando.

Pronouncing Spanish

Don't worry if your pronunciation isn't quite correct.
The important thing is to be willing to try.

The pronunciation guide is based on the Spanish accent used in Latin America. Although it cannot be completely accurate, it certainly will be a great help.

• Read the guide as naturally as possible, as if it were English.

• Put stress on the letters in *italics*, e.g. pap-*ah*.

If you can, ask a Spanish-speaking person to help and move on as soon as possible to speaking the words without the guide.

Words Las palabras
lass pal-*abrass*

left

a la izquierda

ah lah iss-kee*airdah*

right

a la derecha

ah lah dair-*aycha*

hair
el pelo
el *pay*-lo

face
la cara
lah *kah*ra

eyes
los ojos
loss ohoss

cheek
la mejilla
la me*hee*yah

ears
las orejas
lass *oreh*-hass

chin
el mentón
el ment*on*

nose
la nariz
lah nar*eess*

neck
el cuello
el *kweh*-yo

teeth
los dientes
loss dee-*entess*

head
la cabeza
ah ka*beh*-sah

shoulder
el hombro
el *om*bro

back
la espalda
ah ess*pal*dah

toes
los dedos
del pie
loss *deh*-doss del pee-*eh*

What a sight!
¡Qué espectáculo!
keh ess-pec*ta*-koolo

What a mess!
¡Qué lío!
keh *lee*-oh

What a smell!
¡Qué olor!
keh olor

talcum powder
el talco
el *ta*lko

baby
el bebé
el be*beh*

perfume
el perfume
el pair-*foo*meh

story
el cuento
el *kw*ento

bedroom
el dormitorio
el dohr-mee-*toh*-reeoh

bathroom
el cuarto de baño
el *kwa*rto deh *ban*yo

A simple guide to pronouncing this Spanish story

Apúrate, Molly
ap-oorateh, *mollee*

"Vamos Molly, al cuarto de baño.
*b*amoss *mollee*, al *kwa*rto deh *ban*yo

Después te leeré un cuento", dice papá.
*d*ess-*pwes* teh le*here*h oon *kwen*to *dee*-seh pap-*ah*

"¡Llévame en brazos, llévame en brazos!"
*y*eh-vameh en *brah*-soss, *y*eh-vameh en *brah*-soss

Papá toma a Molly.
*p*ap-*ah* *t*omah ah *mollee*

"¿Cabeza abajo?"
*c*a*beh*-sah a*bah*o

"¿Sobre mis hombros?"
*s*obreh meess *o*mbross

"¿O en mi espalda?" pregunta papá.
*o*h en mee ess*pal*dah, preg-*oo*ntah pap-*ah*

"¡Como un bebé!" dice Molly, riendo.
*c*om-oh oon be*beh*, *dee*-seh *mollee*, ree-*en*do

"Apúrate, Molly", dice papá.
*a*p-*oo*rateh, *mollee*, *dee*-seh pap-*ah*

"Te espero en tu dormitorio".
*t*eh ess*pair*o en too dormee-*toh*-reeoh

"Lávate la cara", llama,
*l*ahvah-teh lah *kah*ra, *yah*mah

y detrás de las orejas".
e deh-*trass* deh lass *oreh*-hass

"Cepíllate los dientes".
*s*epee*y*ateh loss *dee*-entess

Molly se cepilla el pelo también.
*m*ollee seh se*pee*yah el *pay*-lo tamb-*yen*

a la izquierda…
*a*h lah iss-*kee*airdah

…a la derecha,
*a*h lah dair-*ay*chah

…sobre la nariz,
*s*obreh lah nar*eess*

y todo encima de la cabeza!
e todo en*see*mah deh lah ka*beh*-sah

Molly se mira en el espejo de papá.
mollee seh *meer*ah en el es*peh*-ho deh pap-*ah*

Su mentón es largo,
soo men*t*on ess *lar*-go

…sus ojos son grandes,
sooss *o*hoss son *grand*ess

…sus mejillas son gorditas.
sooss me*hee*yass son gor*deet*ass

¡Qué espectáculo!
keh ess-pecta-*k*oolo

Se pone talco en la mano y sopla…
seh *p*oneh *tal*ko en lah *mah*-no ee *s*oplah

…¡y sopla!
ee *s*oplah

¡Qué lío!
keh *lee*-oh

Se echa perfume en el cuello…
seh *eh*-chah pair-*foo*meh en el *kweh*-yo

…y en los dedos del pie.
ee en loss *deh*-doss del pee-*eh*

¡Qué olor!
keh olor

Molly se acuerda de repente de su papá.
mollee seh a*kwair*dah deh re*pen*teh deh soo pap-*ah*

"¡Ya vengo, papá!" llama.
*y*ah *b*engo pap-*ah*, *yah*mah

¿Pero adivina lo que Molly encuentra
*p*airoh a*deev*eenah loh keh *mollee* en*kwen*trah

en su dormitorio?
en soo dormee-*toh*-reeoh

"¡Papá, despiértate! ¡Quiero un cuento!"
pap-*ah* dess-pee*air*tateh, *kee*airo oon *kwen*to

**Pero él está profundamente dormido
y roncando.**
*P*airo el estah pro*foon*-damenteh dor*mee*do
ee ron*k*ando